BUSY DAY

A BOOK OF ACTION WORDS

By Betsy and Giulio Maestro

Crown Publishers, Inc., New York

10 9 8 7 6 5 4 3 2 1

The text of this book was set in 24 pt. Century Schoolbook.
The three-color illustrations were prepared as black line and wash drawings
with half-tone overlays, prepared by the artist, for yellow and pink.

Library of Congress Cataloging in Publication Data
Maestro, Betsy.   Busy day.   Summary: Activities surrounding a day at the circus illustrate such action words as pulling, marching, waving, laughing, and washing.   1. English language—Verb—Juvenile literature. 2. English language—Gerund—Juvenile literature. [1. English language—Verb. 2. Circus stories]   1. Maestro, Giulio. II. Title.   PE1271.M3 1978   [E]   77-15635
ISBN 0-517-53288-3

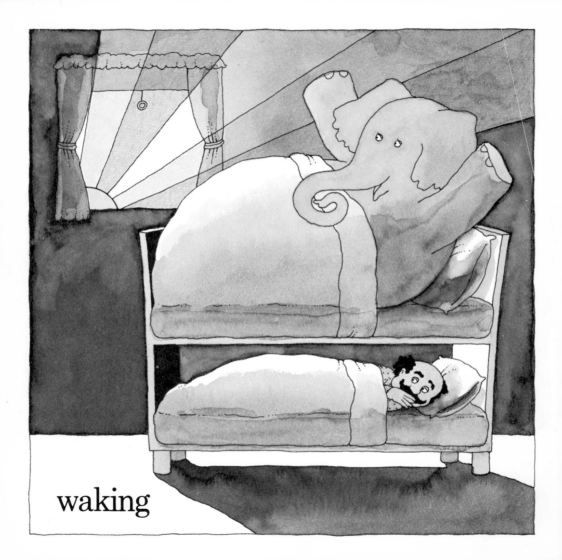

waking

washing

dressing

eating

working

pushing

pulling

painting

reading

running

marching

sitting

climbing

swinging

jumping

falling

crying

crawling

hiding

laughing

swimming

dancing

leaping

hopping

waving

walking

resting

playing

sleeping